Lot the Tot and the Super Hero

AuthorHouse™
1663 Liberty Drive
Bloomington, IN 47403
www.authorhouse.com
Phone: 1 (800) 839-8640

Because of the dynamic nature of the Internet, any web addresses or links contained in this book may have changed since publication and may no longer be valid. The views expressed in this work are solely those of the author and do not necessarily reflect the views of the publisher, and the publisher hereby disclaims any responsibility for them.

This book is printed on acid-free paper.

ISBN: 978-1-7283-3903-0 (sc)
ISBN: 978-1-7283-3902-3 (e)

Library of Congress Control Number: 2019920177

Print information available on the last page.

Published by AuthorHouse 12/12/2019

authorHOUSE

Lot the Tot and the Super Hero

Written and Illustrated by
Sandra C. Saenz

Today is no ordinary day. Super Lot is busy saving the world from all the bad guys!

Super Lot has many superpowers that make him a very powerful super hero.

He is the strongest super hero in the universe!

Wobble, Wobble

Super Lot is so fast, he can leave a turtle in his dust!

Zap!

With his X-ray vision, he can see through the dirtiest window imaginable.

"I am so proud of you! You make an awesome super hero," mama laughs. "Let me tell you about the most powerful super hero of all," mama says with a smile.

"He has many superpowers and He always saves the day!" Daddy cheers as he lifts Super Lot up high in the sky.

"This super hero's name is Jesus! He sees all things, knows all things and is everywhere at once," mama giggles as she joins in on the fun.

"Yes. Jesus has many superpowers, but the greatest power of all is His power to save us. He does this because He died on the cross for all our sins," Daddy chuckles.

Forever!

"He is so powerful and loving, that when we put our trust in Him, He promises to take us to heaven with Him forever!" Mama and Daddy cheer with excitement.

Lot has always wanted to be a super hero that fights bad guys and saves the day with his superpowers.

But today, Lot is thankful that he knows Jesus, the most powerful and loving super hero of all!

Printed in the United States
By Bookmasters